CW00865107

Also available in Spanish
' La Bailarina Estrellada'
and Welsh
'Y Ddawnswraig Serennog'.

Paperback – Ebook – Audiobook

Search Amazon or go to
smileymindskids.com

The Starlit Dancer

The magical bedtime story of a girl
whose love lights up the world!

By Maggie Richards

Every night, something magical
and mysterious unfolds in
Mabel's bedroom.

It happens at the same time.
In the same way.
Every day.

And tonight is no exception...

At 11.59pm – that's one minute to midnight – Mabel quietly wakes from her sleep.

She sits up, smiles, stretches her arms, and quietly gets out of bed.

First her right foot finds the floor. Then her left.

Softly, sleepily, silently, she pads her way along the carpet to the centre of her sanctuary.

Wise as an owl, Mabel stands still now, closes her precious eyes .
And waits...

One... Two... Three... Four... Five...
Six... On the seventh second there
it is! She hears it!

Mabel hears the magical musical
band in her mind beginning to play.
Hurray!

It's a waltzy, whirly, wonderful
tune by who she cannot say.

Up jump Mabel's toes!
Up go her knees!
Up float her arms!
Flowing and spinning
As if covered in charms
She dances and dances
And whirls and swirls
Until there's no more girl
Only the twirl!

On and on Mabel dances. Every swirly twirl fills her with glee until a part of her, one we cannot see, flies totally, totally, totally free!

Up, up, up it journeys to the stars on high and dances among them across the sparkling night sky!

Ha
ha
ha!

Some magical minutes pass before Mabel hears "Stop!" sound softly in her mind.

The voice is ever so kind.

She stops... And lets out the loveliest laugh: *Ha ha ha!*

Now the sparkling stars seize their chance. They love Mabel so much that they race down from the Heavens and dance straight into her heart!

Whoosh!

Weeee!

Swish!

Such bliss you *cannot* miss!

There they soar again!

Back up to their peaceful place in space.

If you look closely you'll see the stars
are a little twinklier now that they've
played with their friend.

Mabel goes back to bed now, under
the duvet, and rests her head.

Her heart is filled with peace.

From the soothing silence in her
mind she hears the sweetest whisper:
"You are the Starlit Dancer.
When you whirled,
you lit up the world!"

- - -

Also from the Smiley Minds team...

Available now on iTunes,
Amazon and more.
smileymindskids.com